Wings

of the

Fallen

Dragon Riders of Osnen Prequels
Book 2

OTHER BOOKS

Dragon Riders of Osnen

The Price of Honor
Trial by Sorcery
A Bond of Flame
The Warrior's Call
The Coin of Souls
Wing of Terror
Eyes of Stone
Tooth and Claw
The Servant of Souls
Smoke and Shadow
The Dark Rider
The Song of Bones
Sword and Crown
Tides of Darkness
Wrath and Ruin
Tomb of Oaths

Marked by the Dragon

Scale of the Dragon
Egg of the Dragon
Call of the Dragon
Wrath of the Dragon

The Fallen King Chronicles

Dragonsphere
The Fallen King
The Valiant King
The Restored King

Wings

of the

Fallen

Dragon Riders of Osnen Prequels
Book 2

RICHARD FIERCE

Dragonfire Press

e-Book ISBN: 979-8-89631-048-8

Print ISBN: 979-8-89631-049-5

CONTENTS

Chapter 1   1

Chapter 2   8

Chapter 3   18

Chapter 4   24

Chapter 5   31

Chapter 6   38

Chapter 7   45

Chapter 8   52

Chapter 9   61

Chapter 10   69

Chapter 11   75

Chapter 12   81

Chapter 13   88

Chapter 14   100

Chapter 15   109

1

THE CLANG OF STEEL rang out as Matthias Baines parried a mock blow. The training grounds of the Citadel were alive with the din of combat, each member honing their skills against constructed foes made of straw and wood. Matthias ducked and weaved between his adversaries, his sword a blur of motion. Sweat glistened on his brow, and the early morning sun cast slanted shadows across the courtyard where the riders trained.

"Keep your guard up, Alton!" Matthias called out.

He pivoted on his heel, dispatching another imaginary enemy with a decisive thrust. His fellow guards rallied to the call, their formation tight as they pushed forward, advancing against an unseen force.

"Form up," he commanded sharply.

Together, they moved as one entity, their shields interlocking with one another. Matthias's ice blue eyes scanned the field. A wooden adversary charged, its mechanism whirring. With a shout, he broke rank, engaging the construct with a series of swift strikes that left it dismantled on the ground.

"Enough!"

The booming voice cut through the fray, halting the clatter of weapons and the shouts of exertion. Curate Aric, a towering figure clad in burnished armor, strode onto the field. His gaze swept over the riders, all of them panting and looking at him expectantly.

"Matthias," Aric said, his eyes locking onto the man. Matthias straightened, his chest heaving as he awaited the curate's judgment. "Your performance today was exceptional. You've shown not just skill but the heart of a true dragon rider. Bravery and loyalty are the pillars upon which our brotherhood stands, and you, lad, have them in spades."

Pride swelled within Matthias's chest, and a warmth that combated the chill of the morning air swept over him. Curate Aric's praise was not given lightly, and to receive such commendation from a man he admired stirred something within him he hadn't felt since the birth of his son.

"Thank you, sir," Matthias replied breathlessly, adrenaline still coursing through his veins. "I serve at the pleasure of the Order and the Citadel."

"Indeed, you do." Aric's stern expression softened into a rare smile as he placed a heavy hand on Matthias's shoulder. "Keep this up, and I foresee a bright future for you within our ranks."

Around them, the other guards nodded in agreement, their faces etched with respect and a hint of envy. Matthias felt the weight of their expectations, but it was a burden he was ready to bear. He had vowed to protect the kingdom and his fellow riders, and it was not an oath he took lightly. But more than that, he wanted his wife and son to be proud of him and his accomplishments.

"Back to it, then," Curate Aric commanded, releasing Matthias.

With a final nod, Matthias rejoined his companions. He resumed his exercise, his movements full of renewed vigor.

—

Matthias's muscles ached with a satisfying burn as he strode toward the stable. He nodded to the men on watch at the entrance of the underground cave and continued inside, the stone beneath his boots rough and uneven. The clash of swords and the shouts of training exercises faded behind him, replaced by the calmer sounds of dragons stirring within their caves.

Hello Valkyra, Matthias greeted as he approached his dragon's alcove. Her blue scales glittered under the torchlight, making it appear as though she were glowing. At the sound of his voice, the dragon lifted her head, her piercing eyes focusing on him.

Matthias extended a hand to gently stroke the smooth ridge of her snout. Valkyra responded with a low rumble that resonated through the air, vibrating against Matthias's palm. They shared a moment of quiet understanding, a silent conversation between rider and dragon, each basking in the other's presence.

Valkyra nuzzled his hand, her breath warm. She had been more than just a mount to Matthias; she was his companion, his confidant, the wings upon which his courage soared. Together they had forged an unbreakable bond through trials and triumphs alike. He loved Valkyra, dearly so. He loved his family, too, but the love he had for Valkyra was something else entirely.

Their tranquil moment was shattered by the urgent tolling of the Citadel's belltower. A deep, sonorous sound that signaled imminent danger. Matthias stiffened, his heart racing as he recognized the call to arms—an alarm not heard in years.

One of the guards from outside rushed into view. "The border villages are under siege!"

"By who?" Matthias asked.

"Midia!"

Curate Aric entered the stable, his stern expression silently reprimanding the guard's panicked news.

"Saddle up," Aric ordered. "We leave immediately."

The stable erupted into chaos. Matthias grabbed Valkyra's harness from the hook on the wall and began strapping it onto her.

Are you ready? he asked.

I am always ready.

Valkyra spread her wings wide, knocking over a stack of hay. She reared up slightly, her body tensing like a coiled spring.

Matthias secured the last buckle and hoisted himself onto her back. His gaze swept over the flurry of activity around them. The riders were mobilizing with impressive speed, each of them driven by the same sense of duty that coursed within him.

Valkyra stomped out of the stable and into the courtyard, issuing a thunderous roar. The clarion call was answered by several other dragons, and Matthias's heart thundered in his chest, mirroring the heavy footsteps of dragons that soon filled the air. His fellow riders were a whirlwind of motion around him, each one armed with a lance or a sword. Matthias's own blade was sheathed at his waist, the weight of it providing a small measure of comfort.

Valkyra snorted, a plume of smoke rising from her nostrils. Her scales gleamed like polished sapphires under the sunlight, and Matthias couldn't help but admire his dragon's beauty.

"Move out!" Aric shouted, redirecting his focus.

With a powerful leap, Valkyra surged into the sky, which became a maelstrom of color and sound as the other riders took flight. They realigned mid-air, getting into formation. Matthias gripped the saddle horn tightly and turned his gaze toward the border.

While he was glad for the excitement, he prayed they weren't going to war.

2

THE SKY WAS A cacophony of flapping wings and roars. Smoke billowed up from the ground, the land scorched by dragon flame. The Midians had soldiers on the ground and in the air, and their griffons shrieked loudly as they battled with the Osnen riders.

Valkyra banked sharply to the left, passing near a group of griffons. Matthias's sword sliced through the air, finding its mark in the gaps of an enemy's armor. The soldier's eyes widened in surprise before he slipped free of the saddle and fell to his death. Matthias's short brown hair was matted with sweat and grime, sticking to his forehead beneath his helmet. He deftly parried a lance aimed for his chest, countering with a thrust that sent the man backward, crashing hard against the back of his griffon.

Around him, the battle raged on, the riders outnumbered but holding their own. With every beat of her powerful wings, Valkyra weaved through the aerial melee, her fiery breath carving paths of destruction through the enemy's forces. The smell of burnt flesh stung Matthias's nostrils, but he ignored the stench and continued striking at any enemy who came within range.

"Hold the line!" Curate Aric shouted, his voice cutting through the din.

Matthias was glad to be fighting by the man's side. Even as the odds stacked ever higher against them, Aric's resolve did not waver. His dragon moved with a grace that belied his bulk, each slash of his claws measured and precise, conserving energy for the long fight ahead. Aric's movements were equally deadly, honed through years of rigorous training, now on full display as he defended not just his own life but the lives of his brothers-in-arms.

They need help, Valkyra said.

Matthias scanned the ground and spotted a few people fleeing, a contingent of Midian soldiers chasing after them. He eyed the formation of the riders and was confident they wouldn't be overtaken if he broke away.

Take us down, he told Valkyra.

She tucked her wings in and sped toward the ground, pulling up at the last moment.

Matthias leaped from the saddle and hit the ground running, intercepting the soldiers. He dodged a spray of earth as Valkyra landed heavily nearby, her claws gouging deep furrows in the soil. Matthias drove back an opponent who had sought to exploit the momentary distraction.

His bravery was not just for show, nor was it reckless. He sought to protect the innocent, and he feared if the Midians won here, they would rampage across Osnen unchecked before the Citadel rallied the rest of the riders. That thought drove him onward, and he dispatched three men before Valkyra flamed the rest.

The people who fled were safely away, and he climbed back into the saddle just as a cry sliced through the cacophony of battle. Matthias turned sharply, his gaze locking onto the source. Curate Aric and his dragon had landed on the ground and a group of Midian soldiers were converging on them. The seasoned rider fought valiantly, but the press of bodies threatened to overwhelm him, and his dragon was beset on all sides.

Without hesitation, Matthias mentally shouted to Valkyra, *To Aric, now!*

The dragon responded instantly, her powerful muscles propelling them forward with breathtaking speed. She bounded ahead, talons outstretched, and snatched a foe about to strike Aric. With a twist of her mighty neck, the threat was neutralized, the soldier tossed aside like a rag doll.

"Riders, to me!" Matthias bellowed, rallying the others even as he fought. They responded to the call, their dragons descending in a protective formation around the Curate.

"Good work," Aric grunted, acknowledging the save with a terse nod before turning to engage an attacker.

"We're not done yet," Matthias called back. They worked together, a storm of wings and valor, a tempest that would not be easily quelled.

A collective roar thundered from the throats of both rider and dragon alike, a sound that melded with the clashing swords and the whooshing of great leathery wings. For a fleeting moment, the tide of battle seemed to turn in their favor as the enemy's advance faltered.

"Push them back!" Aric cried, his voice rising above the clash of arms. His call was met with a surge of concerted effort, riders ushering their dragons into the heart of the fray, flames and steel rending the air. Valkyra's fiery breath cleared a path through the encroaching forces, allowing Aric to rally and orchestrate a counter-offensive.

Matthias could feel hope burgeoning within, a sensation that lifted his spirits even as sweat and grime streaked his face. Valkyra shared in the sentiment, her emotions flooding their bond.

But the reprieve was short-lived.

The enemy, cunning and relentless, had not been idle. As the smoke from Valkyra's breath dissipated, it revealed the Midian forces regrouping with unnerving discipline, their numbers seemingly undiminished. They charged once more, a wave that sought to overwhelm the riders with sheer brute force.

This time, the clash was catastrophic. The ground trembled beneath the onslaught, and the sky darkened with the shadow of the Midian's griffon reinforcements. Matthias fought with a fervor born of desperation, his sword a blur of motion as he parried and struck with lethal precision. Yet for every enemy that fell, two took their place.

He witnessed a fellow rider pulled from the saddle, a cry of anguish lost amidst the chaos. Anger burned within Matthias, fueling his resolve. He wanted to avenge those who had fallen, but this was no mere battle—it was a fight for their very lives.

"For every life they take, we shall repay tenfold!" Matthias yelled.

Valkyra echoed his defiance with a resounding roar, her flames lashing out with renewed ferocity. But even as they fought, the realization that they were being pushed back, inch by harrowing inch, settled heavily upon Matthias's shoulders. He refused to let it break his spirit.

"Fall back!" Aric bellowed. "Riders, fall back!"

Matthias dispatched another enemy and Valkyra flapped her powerful wings as she leaped into the air, quickly ascending above the battlefield. Below, the village now bore the scars of war, its fate hanging in the balance. He knew they could not relent, not while a single breath remained in them to fight.

Smoke unfurled like ghastly ribbons, and Valkyra's wings cut through the acrid air, each beat a somber drumroll to the village's dirge.

Matthias's hands tightened on the reins, his knuckles white as bone against the black leather. Below them, a marketplace had become a roaring inferno, wood and thatch crackling fiercely as the flames consumed them.

"By the gods..." Matthias muttered, his voice barely a whisper.

He could see the silhouettes of dragons against the blaze, desperately trying to stem the tide of Midia's relentless troops. They were like an unending sea of darkness.

"Matthias!" The call came from Larke, a fellow rider whose face was smeared with soot and blood, her expression a grim mask that mirrored his own. "The eastern barricade won't hold!"

His gaze followed her outstretched arm, witnessing the collapse of a defensive wall as Midia's forces poured through the breach like floodwaters through a shattered dam. A cottage crumbled beneath the onslaught, its timbers groaning in protest before succumbing to the violent assault, sending up a plume of ash and embers.

"Retreat!" Aric roared, his command cutting through the turmoil.

A guttural cry rent the air, and Matthias's blood ran cold. He watched helplessly as a dragon and its rider spiraled downwards, their bond severed by a well-aimed spear. The ground rushed up to meet them in a sickening embrace, and Matthias felt something within him shatter.

"Thane," he whispered, the name of his fallen comrade a bitter taste on his lips.

Grief clawed at his chest, a searing pain that rivaled the heat of the very fires that raged below. Thane, who had laughed beside him during their training, who had sworn the same oaths of protection and service to their people, now lay broken amidst the ruins.

"Matthias!" It was Aric's commanding voice that pierced his sorrow, a beacon calling him back to the present. "We must retreat to the Citadel!"

"Retreat?" Matthias echoed, the word foreign, anathema to all he believed in. Yet even as he rebelled against it, he saw the truth etched in the smoke-filled skies: the village was lost.

"We will avenge you," Matthias vowed silently, the vow a promise to those who would no longer rise into the sky. "All of you."

With a heavy heart, he urged Valkyra to follow Curate Aric's orders, their path now one of survival. As they withdrew, the cries of the dying mingled with the roar of dragons, a chorus of agony and defiance that would haunt Matthias long after the battle's end.

"Look out!" Larke's warning cry came just in time. Valkyra veered sharply as a barrage of arrows came towards them, missing her wings by mere inches. Larke's dragon, Icaron, swooped down, incinerating the archers with a blast of flames.

"Close one," Matthias said, offering a quick nod of thanks to her.

"Too close," Larke replied, her eyes scanning the ground for more threats.

Their retreat took them to the safety of the Citadel's high walls, where the remaining dragons landed in the courtyard. The mighty group was now but a shadow of its former self, their numbers half of what they were, faces etched with fatigue and loss.

"Circle up!" Curate Aric's voice boomed across the yard, bringing the scattered riders together. His gaze swept over them, taking in every bruise, every dent in their armor. "We've been dealt a grave blow this day, but there will be time to mourn later.”

“We cannot let Midia claim any more ground,” Matthias said. Valkyra growled in agreement. “We have to strike back—”

“Strategically,” Aric finished for him, the words a reprimand. “Yes, we will retaliate. But first, we need a strategy, one that turns the tide in our favor. I will speak with Master Pevus and the other Curates. For now, everyone should get some rest. I have no doubt we’ll need it.”

Murmurs of assent rippled through the group, yet doubt lingered in the air like the smoke that had chased them from the battlefield. The riders dispersed, some to tend to their dragons, others to seek the solace of rest. Matthias dismounted and turned his gaze to the horizon where the last light of day bled into darkness.

Midia has not seen the last of us, Matthias told Valkyra.

3

THE NEXT MORNING, MATTHIAS awoke early. He went to the training ground and practiced alone. His sleep had been restless, and now he took his frustrations out on the straw dummies. He should have done more, fought harder. The image of Thane falling played continuously in his mind, adding force to his strikes. When he grew tired, he threw his sword down and used the back of his hand to wipe the sweat from his brow.

"Matthias!" a voice called out, echoing throughout the empty courtyard. Matthias turned to see a small group approaching. The one who'd called his name, Curate Henrik, smiled broadly at him. He clasped Matthias on the shoulder in a grip that was both congratulatory and bone-crushing.

"Your valor in battle is becoming the stuff of songs!"

"Only doing my duty, Curate," Matthias replied, the corners of his mouth lifting into a modest smile, even as his chest was heavy with loss. He could feel the weight of eyes upon him, each gaze carrying its own measure of respect.

"Modest as always," Curate Serah chuckled, her dark eyes twinkling with mirth. She stepped forward, offering a respectful nod.

"We heard the stories of your feats yesterday—like a tempest unleashed. You helped save many people. You've earned every bit of praise."

"Thank you, Curate," Matthias said, his spirits lifting. Perhaps he was being too hard on himself.

Curate Aric severed the throng of riders with decisive strides. Matthias's spine stiffened at the sight of him.

"Matthias Baines," Aric's voice resonated with the authority that had weathered countless battles. "Your valor yesterday has not gone unnoticed."

Matthias snapped to attention, his heart hammering in his chest against his ribs. The respect he held for Aric was etched into his very posture, every fiber of his being radiating attentiveness. Aric's gaze swept over him, as if assessing the mettle that had brought Matthias from lowly birth to the vaulted ranks of the Dragon Guard.

"Walk with me," he said, a subtle tilt of his head indicating a more private corner of the courtyard away from prying ears.

They moved in tandem, their boots echoing against stone, until they were shrouded by the shadow of a looming spire. Here, Aric's demeaner shifted, the mask of command giving way to earnest gravity. He leaned closer, and Matthias could smell the leather and steel that clung to the Curate like a second skin.

"Your courage is without question," Aric began in a lowered voice, his eyes searching Matthias's. "But it is your loyalty that I must now call upon. The attack yesterday was orchestrated by Valerius Draven. He proclaims himself king, but he's nothing more than fake royalty. He's taken over Midia, and he poses a great threat to our realm."

Matthias nodded, his jaw set. Now he had a name to direct his anger towards. His hand involuntarily clenched.

"I hope you'll understand the gravity of what I am about to ask. We need intelligence—eyes within enemy lines. Someone to gather information on Valerious's next move."

A flicker of surprise darted across Matthias's face. "You wish... for *me* to undertake this mission?"

"Indeed." Aric gave a slight nod. "It will be perilous. Subterfuge and stealth must be your allies. What you learn could turn the tide of this impending war."

The sun broke over the wall, dissolving the cool embrace of the shadows. Matthias felt the enormity of the task settle upon his shoulders, yet there was no hesitation in his voice when he responded. "I will not fail you, nor the Order."

"Very good," Aric said, a flicker of pride crossing his face. From within his cloak, he produced a sealed scroll. "This contains all you need to know. Depart tonight under the cover of darkness, and may the wind guide you."

Matthias took the scroll, the parchment rough against his fingers. The journey ahead would be a path fraught with danger, but he would tread unflinchingly for the sake of duty.

"You aim to dance with the shadows," a female voice said. Matthias saw Evelyn approaching, one of their physicians. She joined them and smiled. "Even the most adept dancer needs a partner. Curate," she greeted Aric with a nod.

She had been a close friend to Matthias, even before coming to the Citadel. In another life, she may have even been more than that. Her hair was blonde and straight, though it was currently tied back in a ribbon, and her eyes were a striking blue.

"Your healing skills are unmatched," Aric said. "But this task will be perilous. It requires a warrior."

"Which is why you need me to go with him," Evelyn persisted. "Who better to tend wounds in the field than a healer? Besides," she added, her lips curling into a grin as she looked at Matthias. "You need someone to watch your back."

Matthias hesitated, torn between the instinct to protect her and the knowledge that her abilities could mean the difference between life and death. He studied her defiant posture and the look in her eyes and saw more than just a healer; he saw a warrior not unlike himself.

"Your aid would be invaluable," he admitted, glancing at Aric. "But if harm befell her—"

"Then my blood is not on your hands," Evelyn interjected firmly. "I know the risks."

The conviction of her tone brooked no argument, and something in Matthias's heart yielded. He knew he would be stronger with her at his side.

"A companion would be nice," he conceded. "So long as Curate Aric approves?"

They both turned their eyes to him. "It is safer to travel in pairs, and it may help you to keep unwanted attention by appearing as a couple... so long as you don't have any duties pending, I'll speak with Master Pevus and let him know I approved it."

"All of my usual tasks are complete," Evelyn confirmed.

"Very well. Remember, you are to gather information and report back. Don't try to battle the whole of Midia on your own."

Matthias nodded. "Understood."

4

ONCE NIGHT HAD FALLEN and stars pierced the night sky, Matthias met Evelyn in the stable. The scent of hay and dragon musk greeted him, and Valkyra touched his mind as he neared her cave.

Did you get plenty to eat? It might be a while before you have a decent meal.

Valkyra rumbled softly, the sound reverberating off the walls. *I have known hunger before. Do not worry about me.*

Matthias ran a hand along Valkyra's snout. She snorted affectionately, steam rising from her nostrils into the cool air. He checked the saddle straps for any signs of strain while Evelyn packed salves and bandages into the saddlebags. She glanced at him, her blue eyes reflecting the torchlight.

He felt her eyes but ignored her, focusing his attention on running a steel file along one of Valkyra's talons to remove a spur.

I tried chewing that off but it was too small, she said.

Finished with the talon, Matthias hoisted himself onto Valkyra's broad back, careful to distribute his weight evenly. He took a moment to settle in place, adjusting the straps of his saddle. The dragon let out a contented rumble, her enormous wings shifting slightly against her sides. Evelyn followed suit, situating herself behind Matthias.

"You ready?" he asked.

"As ready as I'll ever be," Evelyn replied.

Valkyra exited the cave and headed up the slope that took them into the courtyard. The crisp night air sent a shiver down Matthias's back, and Evelyn stifled her giggle. As the dragon walked, the clinking of Matthia's armor punctuated the stillness of the night. The dragon reached the center of the courtyard and tensed her legs, then pushed off, launching them skyward with a gust of wind that sent loose pebbles skittering across the cobblestones.

The Citadel fell away below as they ascended, its stone walls shrinking until there was nothing visible amidst the shadows. They were in the open expanse of the night sky, and

Matthias lost himself in the cadence of the rhythmic beat of Valkyra's wings.

Evelyn's arms tightened around his waist. "Do you see anything below?" she asked, her voice barely audible over the wind.

Matthias scanned the dark landscape beneath them, searching for any signs of movement or light that might indicate enemy activity. The fields stretched out like a black ocean, broken only by the occasional cluster of trees or distant homestead.

Your eyes are sharper than mine, he said to Valkyra. *Do you see anything to be concerned about?*

The ground is clear.

"Nothing," Matthias called out over his shoulder.

They flew for several hours, passing over the ruins of the town they'd tried to save and across the border into Midia. The canopy of stars stretched endlessly above them, while the shapes of the world below melded into shades of darkness and light. Matthias's gaze remained fixed ahead, his eyelids growing heavy.

As the light of dawn tinged the horizon with color, Evelyn finally broke the silence. "We need to land away from prying eyes, somewhere no one will see your dragon."

Matthias shook off his sleepiness and nodded. A cluster of lights appeared below; a village slowly waking to life. Matthias gestured toward it, and Evelyn followed his line of sight.

"It's as good a place as any to gather information."

Take us down but stay out of range of the town. Evelyn and I will continue ahead on foot.

Valkyra touched down on the outskirts in a heavily wooded area. Matthias dismounted, his boots sinking softly into the dew-covered grass. He offered his hand to Evelyn and helped her down.

Matthias placed a hand on Valkyra's snout. *Stay hidden. If anything happens, fly back to Osnen.*

Valkyra's eyes narrowed, and a puff of warm air escaped her nostrils. *I will not leave you behind,* the dragon replied.

I know you won't, but I'm still going to tell you to anyway. We'll be back as soon as possible.

He patted her scales and turned to Evelyn. "Let's find an inn. We'll get something to eat and keep our ears up."

Together, they walked through the woods toward the town. The sun crested over the hills, casting its warm glow upon them and driving away the chill in Matthias's bones.

The town was a sorry sight. Low, weathered buildings leaned against one another like weary travelers, and the streets were little more than packed dirt, muddied from a recent rain. Smoke rose from a number of the dwellings, and the few people they passed barely acknowledged them.

The inn was located in the center of the town. Its shutters hung crookedly, and a worn sign in front depicted a caravan winding through the mountains. The faded words "The Caravan's Rest" were barely legible.

Matthias pushed open the door, holding it for Evelyn. Inside, the common room was dimly lit by a handful of lanterns and the flickering glow of a hearth. Patrons hunched over their food, their voices low and wary, and the air was thick with the scent of wood smoke and roasted meat.

They found a table by the fire and waited for the innkeeper. A burly man with a salt-and-pepper beard approached, smiling broadly.

"Welcome to my humble establishment," he greeted. "What can I get for you fine travelers?"

"Do you have any rooms available?" Matthias asked.

"Aye, but just one."

Matthias glanced at Evelyn, who nodded her approval.

"We'll take it. And two of your best meals, whatever that might be."

The innkeeper nodded and left, returning shortly with two steaming plates of food. Matthias's mouth watered at the sight of fluffy biscuits smothered in gravy, sausages as long as his fingers, and a heaping pile of scrambled eggs. He took a bite of the biscuit, and the savory, meaty flavor of the gravy danced on his tongue. Matthias savored each bite while listening in to the conversations of the other patrons.

One in particular caught his attention, though it was less a conversation and more an old man raving to himself.

"...dark magic. He's using dark magic to control them, I tell you. They aren't meant to be bent to no man's will." His raspy voice carried the weight of someone who'd seen too much. "The False King," he continued, his hands trembling as he clutched his mug. "His army is going to destroy everything. He'll enslave the great beasts for his evil purposes. It isn't natural."

"I've told you before to stop rambling nonsense in here," the innkeeper said as he walked over to the table the old man was sitting at. "You're scaring my customers."

The man seemed to suddenly realize where he was and mumbled something, casting his gaze around the room.

Evelyn leaned closer to Matthias. "What do you think he's talking about?"

Matthias didn't answer immediately, his brow furrowed in thought as he ate the last of his food. He slid the plate aside and wiped his mouth with his hand.

"There's only one way to find out."

5

AFTER THE INNKEEPER HANDED over the key to their room, Matthias watched the old man carefully, waiting for him to leave. When he finally staggered out of the inn, Matthias and Evelyn followed, keeping their distance. The old man shuffled down the muddy street, muttering under his breath.

When they were far enough from prying eyes, Matthias quickened his pace and called out, "Excuse me, sir. Can we speak with you?"

The old man whirled around, his eyes wild with fear. "Stay back! I know what you are— agents of the False King, sent to silence me!"

Matthias held up his hands in a gesture of peace. "We're not here to harm you. We just want to know more about what you were saying in the inn."

The man's gaze darted between Matthias and Evelyn. "How do I know I can trust you?"

"Because if we were with the False King, you'd already be dead," Matthias said.

The old man hesitated, then nodded slowly. "Fair enough. Not here." He glanced around uneasily. "Too many ears." He led them to a secluded alley, glancing over his shoulder to make sure they weren't followed.

"Tell us everything," Matthias said.

The old man took a deep breath, his eyes shifting nervously. "I escaped from Araphel. I've been a servant there most of my life. The False King... he's using dark magic, experimenting with things no one should ever mess with. He's trying to craft a spell that will bend dragons to his will. It's unnatural, I tell you. He plans to invade Osnen by turning the dragons against their riders."

Matthias and Evelyn exchanged a grim look.

"Do you know when he plans to invade Osnen?"

"As soon as he figures out the spell. Between himself and his sorcerer, it can't be long now."

"How difficult would it be to catch him alone?" Matthias asked.

"The False King? Impossible, I tell you. An army resides at Araphel, and his sorcerer has eyes everywhere." The old man shuddered. "If you had an army of your own, you might have a chance, but even still, you'll need a weapon he can't defend against."

Matthias's mind raced as he absorbed the man's words. The gravity of the situation weighed heavily upon him, knowing that the False King's intentions could bring ruin to Osnen and its people.

"We need to find a way to stop him," Evelyn said.

"There might just be a way, if you're brave enough." The old man lowered his voice and motioned them closer. Matthias scrunched his nose as the stench of sour ale assaulted him.

"There is a place hidden in the mountains beyond Araphel. It's said to hold a weapon of immense power, one that could even defeat the False King's magic."

"What kind of weapon?" Matthias asked, his curiosity piqued.

"A sword forged for the first king of Midia," the old man whispered. "They say it can cleave through enchantments and strike down the mightiest of foes."

"Where can we find this sword?"

"In the ruins of Valen," the old man answered. "But beware, for many have entered seeking its power and never returned."

Matthias thanked him for the information and slipped him a few coins.

"Good luck, rider of Osnen. You'll need it."

"Who said I was a dragon rider?"

"When you've lived as long as I have, there isn't much that escapes your notice."

The man shuffled away, leaving them in the alley.

"We need to warn the Order," Evelyn said. "If the False King manages to control our dragons, the entire kingdom will be in peril."

"We need to find this sword, *then* we can return to inform the Order."

"The False King could launch his attack before we find it. With no warning... it would be a slaughter."

"What good is a warning if we don't have a way to fight back? We need the sword."

"He could have made up the tale of that sword," Evelyn said. "We don't know anything about him."

Matthias clenched his jaw. He was reminded of why nothing had ever happened between them. She constantly challenged him.

"If you want to go back, I'll have Valkyra take you. But I'm staying."

"I'm not leaving you here by yourself, Matthias."

"Then I guess you're coming with me."

They engaged in a staring contest until Evelyn relented. "Fine. We'll do this your way. If the sword doesn't exist, you've wasted our time. And if Osnen is invaded while we're digging around in some blasted ruins, the blood is on your hands."

My hands are already bloody, Matthias thought.

They headed back to the inn, and when they entered the common room, Matthias caught a glimpse of the innkeeper giving them a suspicious glance. He figured the man must have seen them tailing the elderly gentleman, but then he remembered that they hadn't paid for their food or lodging yet.

"My apologies," Matthias said, fishing several coins from the pocket of his cloak. He laid them on the table and added an extra one for good measure. "We were looking for a shop to get some supplies."

The innkeeper's demeanor softened as he pocketed the coins, nodding in approval. "Supplies, eh? Stocking up for a journey?"

Matthias nodded. "Yes. We have a long road ahead of us," he said vaguely, not wanting to reveal too much.

"Where are you headed?"

Matthias stared at the innkeeper as if he could discern the man's intentions. The burly man raised his hands placatingly. "I'm not trying to pry." He leaned in slightly, lowering his voice. "If I may offer a word of advice... beware the forests to the east. Rumors say they're haunted by spirits and creatures of the dark."

"Is Valen to the east?" Evelyn asked.

Matthias shot her a glare but she ignored him.

"Ah, treasure seekers," the innkeeper chuckled. "Normally I can tell by the looks of people. I'll admit I didn't have you two pegged as fortune hunters, but then again, it's been a while since I've seen any come through here. Valen is west of here, about a day's ride on horseback."

"Thank you," Matthias said. "I think we're going to retire to the room for now. We've been on the road a while."

The innkeeper shooed them off with a smile, and Matthias led the way to their room. Once inside, he latched the lock and unbuckled his sword belt.

"What are you doing?" Evelyn asked.

"I'm going to get some sleep. If you want the bed, I'll sleep on the floor."

"We don't have time to sleep! We need to get moving."

Matthias stared at her, trying to be patient. "I'm exhausted. In case you forgot, we left in the middle of the night. If I don't sleep now, we won't make it very far before I doze off."

Evelyn fumed, but she didn't say anything.

"So do you want the bed or the floor?"

6

MATTHIAS AND EVELYN TRAVELED westward on foot, unsure exactly where they needed to go. A merchant caravan was kind enough to point them in the right direction, and after traveling on the main road for roughly an hour, they departed onto an overgrown path. It was obvious the trail had once been well-trodden, but now it was swallowed by twisted roots and thick undergrowth.

Matthias pushed a low-hanging branch out of his way, his boots crunching on fallen leaves. Beside him, Evelyn walked in silence, sweat collecting on her forehead. The air around them felt heavy, and Matthias wished he'd had the foresight to bring lighter clothes.

As they pushed through the thick vegetation, the trees suddenly cleared and they found themselves in a large open field. The ruins of Valen sprawled before them. Massive stone columns, cracked and weathered by time, jutted out of the ground like jagged teeth. Walls lay in heaps of rubble, and creeping vines wound their way over every surface. Despite the decay, an eerie beauty lingered.

"I think this is it," Evelyn said.

"Doesn't look too welcoming," Matthias muttered.

"I don't think it's meant to be. If what that old man said is true, this place is probably riddled with traps. That would explain why no one ever returns."

Matthias scanned the ruins, looking for an entrance. A broken archway loomed ahead, its once intricate carvings now faint and weathered. Strange runes glowed faintly along its surface, their soft blue light barely noticeable. They advanced forward, and Evelyn stopped in front of the archway, her brow furrowed as she studied the symbols.

"Don't touch anything," Matthias warned. "It could be some sort of enchantment."

"I'm not a sorcerer, but I don't think these symbols are magical in nature." She ran a finger over one of the runes, and some of the glowing material was on her finger. "It's sticky like paint. And there's a riddle here," she said, tracing her fingers over the ancient text. Her lips moved silently as she read, her eyes narrowing in thought.

"Well?" Matthias prompted, glancing over his shoulder as if expecting the ruins themselves to rise up against them.

"Patience," Evelyn shot back, though her tone lacked its usual bite. "It says, 'Only the brave of heart and steady of mind may enter. Speak the words that open the path, and prove your worth to claim the sword of kings.'"

Matthias frowned. "And what's that supposed to mean?"

"How should I know? But at least this proves the sword is real."

"Maybe it's a phrase related to Valen? He was the first king of Midia, so that would make sense."

Evelyn shrugged. "This was your idea."

Matthias scowled at her, then wandered the ruins, looking for any clue that could help them unravel the riddle. His eyes landed on a partially crumbled statue with faded inscriptions. Since he wasn't fluent in the Midian language, he called Evelyn over to decipher the words for him.

She brushed away moss and dirt that obscured the engravings and read them aloud,

"'By the will of King Valen, the land shall prosper and its people flourish. His sword, a beacon of hope in the darkest times, shall never falter.'"

Matthias pondered the words, letting them sink in. "'A beacon of hope in the darkest times'... Maybe that's the key."

Evelyn's eyes lit up with understanding. "The words that open the path... 'beacon of hope.' Try saying that to the archway."

Matthias returned to the archway and said, "Beacon of hope."

At first, nothing happened. He looked at Evelyn questioningly, and a low rumble echoed through the ruins as the ground beneath their feet trembled. The scraping of stone filled the air, and the slab in the middle of the archway slid to the side, revealing a steep staircase descending into the earth.

Matthias stared into the dark opening, second guessing his decision to seek out this place. "Why do I get the feeling this is going to be more trouble than it's worth?"

Evelyn stepped toward the opening, glancing at him over her shoulder and offering a faint smile. "You coming?"

Together, they descended into the depths. The staircase spiraled deep into the earth, the air growing warmer and mustier with each step. The faint glow of the runes along the walls was their only light, which made shadows dance on the walls.

When the staircase finally ended, they found themselves in a narrow corridor. The walls were smooth and dark, etched with the same glowing runes that had guided their way. The passage stretched forward, disappearing into the gloom. Matthias took a cautious step forward, his boots scraping against the stone. The sound echoed unnaturally.

"Wait," Evelyn said, grabbing his arm. She crouched low, her fingers brushing the ground. "Look here."

Matthias followed her gaze and saw faint markings on the floor, almost invisible in the dim light. A series of small squares were etched into the stone, arranged in a grid pattern.

"Pressure plates," Matthias murmured. "This whole corridor is probably rigged."

"What happens if we step on the wrong one?"

Matthias gave her a grim look. "Nothing good."

Evelyn pulled a small pouch from her belt and carefully removed a handful of powder. Sprinkling it lightly over the floor ahead, the markings of the pressure plates became clearer. Some squares glowed faintly in response, while others remained dull.

"Clever," Matthias said.

His pulse quickened as he took his first step. The ground beneath him felt solid, but every nerve in his body screamed that danger was near. Evelyn followed close behind, mirroring his steps.

Halfway down the corridor, Matthias's boot scuffed the edge of a glowing square. Instantly, a low grinding noise echoed through the passage. Evelyn froze, her eyes darting upward.

"Get down!" she shouted.

Matthias dropped to the ground as a volley of arrows shot from hidden slits in the walls, whizzing past where his head had been a moment before. One grazed his arm, tearing through the fabric of his sleeve and leaving a shallow cut. He hissed in pain, clutching his arm.

"Let me see it," Evelyn said.

"I'm fine," he replied, shaking off the sting of the wound. "It just took me by surprise."

They continued onward, moving slower now. As they neared the end of the corridor, Matthias's vision began to blur. He leaned against the wall, sweat trickling down his brow.

"What is it?"

Matthias's knees buckled and he slumped to the ground, narrowly missing one of the pressure plates.

"My skin is on fire," he slurred.

"Something's... wrong."

7

"YOU'VE BEEN POISONED," EVELYN SAID.

Matthias felt a surge of panic at her words. Poisoned? The burning sensation spread through his veins, and he struggled to stay conscious. The edges of his vision darkened, and he could feel his heartbeat pounding in his ears.

Evelyn quickly began rummaging through her pack, pulling out vials and herbs in a flurry of motion. Matthias watched her with bleary eyes, his thoughts muddled. The pain intensified, causing his muscles to spasm involuntarily. This couldn't be how he died. Evelyn produced a vial filled with a shimmering red liquid and uncorked it, carefully helping Matthias to drink a small amount.

The effects were almost immediate as the burning sensation in Matthias's veins began to subside, replaced by a cooling sensation spreading through his body.

"Is it helping?"

Matthias nodded weakly. "It's a good thing you came with me."

Evelyn's face softened with relief at his words, though worry still lingered in her eyes. "I couldn't let you go charging into danger alone," she scolded gently, her fingers brushing against his forehead to check his temperature.

Matthias managed a weak smile in response, grateful for her quick thinking and expertise. As the antidote continued to work its magic, color returned to his cheeks and strength flowed back into his limbs. He pushed himself up with Evelyn's assistance.

"Are you able to continue, or should we turn back?"

"I'm not letting a little poison stop me," Matthias replied. "Let's find that sword and get out of here."

As they neared the end of the corridor, the traps became more obvious. A section of the wall began to shift, revealing hidden blades that swiped out in a rhythmic pattern. Matthias timed his movements carefully, darting past the blades and catching Evelyn's hand to pull her through just as they retracted.

Finally, they reached the end of the passage, where a heavy stone door loomed before them. Matthias wiped a droplet of sweat from his face. "That was fun."

Evelyn shot him a sharp look. "This isn't a joke, Matthias. If we're not careful, one of us isn't walking out of here." Her tone softened as she glanced at his injured arm. "Let me check your wound."

Matthias shook his head. "We need to keep moving."

Evelyn forcefully grabbed ahold of his arm and inspected the cut. "It's not deep," she concluded after a moment, "but we need to clean and bandage it properly once we're out of here. The poison was probably the worst part, but it's best to be on the safe side."

Matthias nodded, grateful for her concern despite their volatile relationship. He turned to the door and pushed on it. It was heavy, but it swung open slowly, revealing another dark passage beyond.

Matthias exhaled heavily. "If that was the first trap, I don't want to know what's next."

The corridor beyond the door widened into a cavernous chamber, its walls glittering with embedded crystals that refracted the light of the runes into an array of shifting colors. At the center of the room stood a circular dais, its surface engraved with intricate symbols that pulsed faintly, as though alive. Surrounding the dais were five stone pillars, each bearing a unique emblem carved deeply into their surfaces.

Matthias approached cautiously, his boots echoing against the smooth stone floor. "Let me guess... another trap?"

"Not quite," Evelyn said, her eyes narrowing as she studied the room. She gestured toward the dais. "This looks like a test of wit. The early builders of Midia valued the mind as much as the body."

"How do you know so much about the people of Midia?"

Evelyn's lips quirked into a wry smile. "Let's just say I've had my fair share of adventures and acquired some useful knowledge along the way." She moved closer to the dais, examining the symbols etched into its surface with a focused gaze.

Matthias joined her, his eyes tracing the intricate patterns. "So, what do you think we're supposed to do here?"

"Five paths, five truths. Choose wrongly, and the way is barred. Choose wisely, and the light shall guide you."

The symbols on the dais flared, casting shifting patterns across the walls. Above each pillar, an ethereal light flickered, illuminating the emblems: a sword, a flame, a tree, a star, and a wave.

"What does it mean?" Matthias asked, his brow furrowing.

Evelyn pointed to the symbols on the dais. "Look closely. These markings align with the emblems on the pillars. We need to pair them correctly to proceed."

Matthias squinted at the engravings. Each one depicted a different scene: a warrior brandishing a blade, a forest set ablaze, an ocean storm, a sky full of stars, and a sapling growing in barren soil.

"So it's a matching game," Matthias said.

Evelyn nodded. "The wrong match could trigger a trap, but based on the inscriptions, it seems to imply the door will be sealed behind us."

Matthias grunted. "Locking us in here. Of course."

Evelyn crouched beside the dais, tracing her fingers over the engravings. "The symbols aren't just images; they're representations of values. Courage, destruction, renewal, guidance, and endurance. We need to think about how each emblem aligns with these."

Matthias studied the emblems again. "Courage is the sword," he said after a moment.

"That makes senses to me. Fire represents destruction, obviously. The tree could be renewal—new life growing after devastation. The star likely means guidance, and the wave could be endurance, enduring the storm."

They exchanged a glance, and Evelyn's fingers hesitated over the first symbol. "We'll need to activate these in the right order. If we're wrong…"

Matthias didn't need her to finish the sentence. His hand tightened on his sword hilt. "No pressure, then."

Evelyn touched the engraving of the sword first, then stepped back as the corresponding pillar lit with a soft glow. Nothing happened.

"Good start," Matthias said.

She moved to the flame next, pressing the engraving with a tentative hand. Again, the corresponding pillar glowed. One by one, they activated the symbols: the tree, the star, and finally the wave. When the last symbol was pressed, the chamber fell silent, the light from the pillars fading into darkness.

"Is... that supposed to happen?" Matthias asked, his voice uneasy.

Before Evelyn could answer, the dais began to sink into the floor, revealing a spiraling staircase that descended even further into the earth. The crystals on the walls dimmed, casting the room in shadow.

"It appears we passed," Evelyn said.

Matthias exhaled sharply. "Let's not celebrate just yet."

They descended the new staircase, and Matthias couldn't shake the feeling that the puzzles weren't meant to test their intellect alone—they were meant to wear them down, chipping away at their confidence.

Evelyn glanced at him as they continued into the darkness. "I suspect the next one will be harder," she said softly.

Matthias nodded, his jaw tight. "So be it."

8

THE AIR GREW THICK and heavy as Matthias stepped into the chamber. It was smaller than the others, a circular room enclosed by walls that shimmered like liquid silver. There were no runes, no visible exits—only a suffocating silence.

"Evelyn?" Matthias called, turning to where she had been standing a moment ago.

But she was gone.

"Evelyn!" he shouted. His voice echoed back at him as though the room itself was mocking him.

He spun in place, his heart pounding. The silver walls began to ripple, distorting his reflection. Shadows coalesced, swirling around him like smoke before condensing into a solid form.

A deep voice filled the space. "You cannot hide from what lies within."

Matthias drew his sword, the blade trembling in his grip. "Show yourself!"

The shadows shifted again, morphing into a scene so vivid it made Matthias stagger back a step. He was no longer in the chamber but standing in the familiar warmth of his family's farmhouse. The scent of fresh bread and pinewood filled the air, and sunlight streamed through the windows.

For a moment, Matthias was frozen, his breath caught in his throat.

"Matthias!" His younger sister, Liana, came running toward him, her laughter echoing through the house. She was as he remembered her, her golden hair shining in the light. Behind her, his mother stood by the hearth, stirring a pot, while his father sharpened tools at the table.

"Liana?" Matthias whispered, lowering his sword.

But something was wrong. The sunlight dimmed, and the air grew cold. The laughter faded, replaced by a distant rumble like thunder. Matthias's parents turned to him, their faces pale and gaunt, their eyes hollow.

"Why didn't you save us?" his mother said, her voice brittle and cracking like dry leaves.

Matthias staggered back. "What? No... I—"

The walls of the farmhouse dissolved into smoke, revealing a battlefield drenched in blood. The screams of the dying filled the air, and dragons wheeled above, their roars shaking the earth. At the center of it all, Matthias stood, his armor slick with blood, his sword heavy in his hand.

Before him lay his wife and son, their bodies broken and lifeless.

"No!" Matthias cried, dropping to his knees. He reached for them, but the ground beneath him turned to ash, swallowing them whole.

The shadowy voice returned, circling him like a predator. "You fear failure. You fear losing those you love. You tell yourself you fight for them, but will they ever forgive the blood on your hands?"

Matthias clenched his fists, his knuckles white. "This isn't real. This is a trick!"

"Is it?" the voice taunted. "Or is it the truth you refuse to face?"

The battlefield melted away, replaced by a void of endless darkness. From the shadows stepped a figure—himself.

The doppelgänger's eyes burned with a cold, merciless light. "You can't protect them," it said, its voice an icy mirror of his own. "Every step you take leads them closer to ruin. The more you fight, the more you destroy."

Matthias gritted his teeth, his hand tightening around his sword. "I fight to protect them. To make a better world for them."

The shadow version of himself smirked, raising its own blade. "Prove it."

The doppelgänger lunged, and Matthias barely had time to parry the strike. Their swords clashed, the sound ringing through the void like a bell. Blow after blow came, each strike forcing Matthias back.

"You're weak," the shadow spat, its movements fluid and relentless. "You'll never be enough."

Matthias's arms ached, his breath coming in ragged gasps. The shadow forced him to his knees, its blade pressing against his throat.

"Admit it," it whispered. "You'll fail them, just as you failed your brother."

Matthias froze, the words striking deeper than any blade. His mind flashed to his brother's face, the memory of that fateful day when he hadn't been fast enough, strong enough, to save him.

Tears burned in his eyes, but he shook his head. "No. I won't let the past define me. I've made mistakes, but I fight because I must. Because it's the only way to honor their memory."

With a roar, Matthias surged upward, his sword slicing through the shadow. The figure dissolved into smoke, and the oppressive darkness lifted.

The silver walls of the chamber reappeared, and Matthias found himself standing alone once more. His chest heaved, and sweat dripped from his brow.

The voice echoed one final time, softer now. "You have faced your fear and found your truth. The path is open."

The outline of a doorway appeared, faint at first, but it solidified as Matthias approached. Beyond it, he could see Evelyn slumped against the wall, her face pale.

Matthias ran to her, kneeling at her side. "Evelyn!"

Her eyes fluttered open, and she gave him a weak smile. "You made it."

"*We* made it," Matthias said, his voice firm.

He helped her to her feet, supporting her weight as they continued ahead. The passage was narrow and treacherous, carved from ancient stone that crumbled at the edges.

Matthias supported Evelyn as best he could, her weight heavy against him.

"What happened to you? One moment you were there, and the next you were gone."

"I was in some sort of labyrinth, and I didn't see the trap in front of me. You vanished, and I was too focused on trying to find you. Once I realized the danger, I couldn't move quick enough to avoid the trap."

Blood seeped through the makeshift bandage wrapped around her leg. Her breathing was shallow, and her skin was turning pale. "I'll be fine," she murmured, though her voice lacked its usual strength.

"Not without help you won't be," Matthias replied firmly, his jaw tight as he scanned the dark corridor for a safe place to rest.

"I've been hurt worse." Her smile was faint, tinged with pain. "Don't stop on account of me."

Matthias ignored her protest, guiding her toward a small alcove where the floor was smooth enough to sit. The faint light of the chamber illuminated the strain in her features.

"You're staying here until I take care of that wound," he said, lowering her gently to the ground.

Evelyn gritted her teeth as he removed the bandage. The sight of the injury made Matthias's stomach turn. It was deep, and blood pooled in the gaping wound. He rifled through her supplies, pulling out a salve and fresh bandages.

"Stay still," he ordered, though his touch was gentle as he worked.

Evelyn hissed through her teeth when he applied the salve. "You're surprisingly good at this."

"Valkyra gets herself hurt more often than you'd think," Matthias replied, focusing on his task. "Dragons don't complain as much, though."

That earned him a weak chuckle. "You'd be surprised. I've heard some dragons are worse than humans."

The humor faded as Matthias tied off the bandage, and Evelyn's gaze met his. "Don't let me slow you down. If you need to leave me here—"

"No." His voice was resolute, cutting her off.

Evelyn blinked, startled by the intensity in his tone.

"I'm not abandoning you."

Evelyn's expression softened, her voice quieter. "It's not about abandoning me. It's about doing what's necessary."

"What's necessary is keeping both of us alive," Matthias said. "I'll carry you if I have to."

Evelyn studied him for a moment, her lips curving into a faint smile. "You've changed, you know."

Matthias frowned. "What do you mean?"

"You're more confident," she said, leaning back against the stone wall. "When you first came to the school, you were so wrapped up in your fears—of failing, of not being good enough. But now... I see it in the way you carry yourself, the way you make decisions. You're not the same man who walked into the Citadel."

Matthias hesitated, the weight of her words settling over him. She was right. The trials he'd faced forced him to confront parts of himself he'd tried to ignore—his doubts, his fears, his guilt. And while those feelings hadn't disappeared, he'd found something stronger beneath them: resolve.

He sighed. "Maybe I have changed. But I'm still not leaving you behind."

Evelyn nodded. "Good, because I'd hate to have to crawl after you."

Matthias smirked. After ensuring she was as comfortable as possible, he stood and adjusted his sword belt. He glanced down at her.

"Rest here. I'll scout the way ahead and make sure it's clear."

9

A CHAMBER LOOMED AHEAD, its massive stone doors carved with intricate patterns of griffons flying among the stars. Matthias's footsteps echoed in the corridor as he approached, his heart pounding.

Evelyn leaned on his shoulder. Her face was still pale, but the color was starting to return. Her injury slowed her pace, but it wasn't stopping her. She glanced at Matthias, her eyes sharp despite her exhaustion. "This is it."

"How do you know?"

Evelyn brushed her fingers against the weathered carvings on the doors. "It says beyond this door lies the 'power of Valen.' That must be the sword."

Matthias stared at the doors, wondering if another test awaited them inside. "It's probably been sealed for centuries," he said.

"And we'll be the first to step inside... the first to claim the sword."

Matthias steeled himself and pushed against the doors. A faint hum filled the air. The patterns on the stone began to glow, lines of light tracing the intricate carvings until the entire surface radiated a soft, silver aura. The doors groaned as they parted, revealing the chamber beyond.

The room was vast, its ceiling lost in shadow. Pillars of crystal rose from the floor, casting shimmering light across the walls. At the center stood a raised platform, and on it rested a sword.

Matthias and Evelyn approached cautiously, their footsteps muffled by the thick layer of dust coating the floor. The weapon was unlike anything Matthias had imagined. Its blade was forged from an unknown metal that shimmered with a prismatic sheen. At its head was a griffon's claw clutching an orb of swirling light.

"You found it," Evelyn whispered, her voice tinged with awe. "The sword of the first king of Midia. It's beautiful."

Matthias stared at the sword, its power almost tangible. He felt its pull, as though it recognized him, called to him. But as he reached for it, Evelyn's hand shot out, gripping his arm.

"Wait," she said, her voice sharp.

Matthias froze. "What is it?"

"There's no way this weapon is unguarded."

"What do you mean? We just passed the tests to get here. Surely there's nothing else in the way."

As if in answer to her warning, the air around them shifted. The light dimmed, and a deep rumble resonated through the chamber. Matthias instinctively stepped in front of Evelyn as a figure materialized on the platform.

It was a ghostly apparition, a man clad in shimmering armor, his eyes glowing with an otherworldly light. He held a sword identical to the one on the platform, his expression grave.

"Who dares to claim the sword?" the figure demanded, his voice echoing as though it came from the walls themselves.

Matthias squared his shoulders, meeting the figure's gaze. "I am Matthias Baines of Osnen. We seek the weapon to stop the False King."

The guardian studied him for a moment, his ethereal eyes piercing his very soul. "This blade is not meant for the unworthy. It is a burden as much as it is a gift. To wield it is to sacrifice. Do you understand this?"

Matthias hesitated, the weight of the guardian's words sinking in. "I do," he said finally. "If that's what it takes to save my people, then I will bear it."

The guardian's gaze shifted to Evelyn, his expression unreadable. "And you? Do you stand beside him willingly, knowing the dangers this path brings?"

Evelyn straightened despite her injury, her voice firm. "I do. We've come this far together, and we're not turning back now."

The guardian nodded, a flicker of approval crossing his face. "Very well. But the sword does not choose lightly. One final question remains: Are you willing to give all that you are to protect this world?"

Matthias's throat tightened. He thought of his family, his home, the lives that depended on him. And then he thought of Evelyn, wounded but unwavering.

"I am," he said. "I'll give everything if I need to."

The guardian smiled and stepped aside, gesturing to the blade. "Then it is yours. May your heart remain pure, and your will unbroken."

As the apparition faded, the chamber grew still once more. Matthias approached the platform, his fingers trembling as he reached for the sword. The moment his hand closed around the hilt, a surge of energy shot through him, filling him with warmth and light. The orb at the staff's head flared brightly, and for a moment, Matthias felt as though he could hear the heartbeat of the world itself.

Evelyn watched him, her expression a mix of curiosity and pride. "You did it."

Matthias turned to her, the sword glowing faintly in his hand. "*We* did it," he corrected.

But deep in his chest, he felt the weight of the guardian's words. The sword was his now, but it came with a price—one he knew he would have to pay.

The soft glow of the sword's orb illuminated the dim corridor as Matthias and Evelyn made their way back through the ruins of Valen. Evelyn leaned against the crumbling wall for support, her steps slower than usual. Matthias glanced at her. "How's the wound?"

"It's fine," she replied, though her voice was thin. "I'll manage."

"You don't have to," Matthias replied, shifting the sword to his other hand and offering his arm. "Let me help."

Evelyn hesitated but relented, leaning on him as they continued forward. As they neared the exit, Valkyra's presence touched Matthias's mind. It was faint due to the distance between them, but he could sense her pride at his success.

We're on our way back, Matthias told the dragon.

When they emerged into the open air, the ruins behind them seemed smaller and less foreboding. The sky was a welcome sight, and the warmth of the sun on his skin eased the tension that had settled in Matthia's bones.

They paused at the edge of the ruins to give Evelyn a moment to rest. She sat on the ground and closed her eyes.

"Are you all right?" Matthias asked.

"I will be, but I don't think I can make it back to the inn."

"I'm not leaving you here, so don't ask me to again."

"You can't carry me that far. And I wouldn't let you even if you could."

Matthias reached out to Valkyra. *I know it's risky, but I need you to come to us. Evelyn was injured and can't walk.*

I've grown bored hiding in the trees. I'm on my way.

Valkyra arrived as the sun was beginning to descend beyond the horizon. She landed among the ruins and lowered her head as Matthias approached, her eyes locking onto the sword.

So this is the weapon, she said, her mental tone curious. *It feels... ancient. Powerful.*

I'm sure it is, Matthias said, lifting the blade slightly. The sword responded, its orb glowing faintly as if acknowledging the dragon's attention.

Evelyn got up on her own, her face twisted in agony. She limped over to where Matthias was and pushed his hand away as he offered to help her. "We need to decide our next move. The False King won't stop, and now that we have this..." She gestured to the sword. "We have a way to fight him."

"Then we stop running. We take the fight to him."

Evelyn's brow furrowed. "You're serious?"

"Yes," Matthias said. "Curate Aric's instructions were to learn what we could and report back. We know what the False King is plotting, so I think we should return to the Citadel. When the Order hears what we have to say, I think they'll want to strike at him before he can strike us. And having found this weapon is an added bonus."

Valkyra rumbled her approval. Matthias placed a hand on her scales, rubbing them comfortingly. "The sun is going down now. We can wait until it's dark, and head back unseen."

Evelyn nodded. "All right. But first, let's eat something. I'm starved."

Matthias gathered some fallen branches from the woods and stacked them into a pile. Valkyra breathed her flames onto the wood, igniting a fire. They sat near the blaze and ate some of the food they'd purchased at the village.

Once night fell over the landscape, Matthias helped Evelyn climb onto Valkyra's back, then secured the sword in a sheath strapped to his saddle before climbing up and sitting behind Evelyn. The dragon spread her wings, and with a mighty leap, they took to the air, speeding toward Osnen.

10

THE WALLS OF THE Citadel had never looked so imposing—or so welcoming. Valkyra landed with a graceful thud in the central courtyard, her massive wings stirring the cold morning air and scattering dust and loose stones.

Matthias dismounted first, then helped Evelyn as she slid down. She favored her injured side but masked her discomfort with practiced ease. A stable hand approached and offered to take Valkyra's reins.

"Thank you," Matthias said. "Please make sure she gets fresh meat and water."

The dragon snorted, sending a puff of warm air into the boy's face. *I'll handle myself,* Valkyra said, her tone laced with amusement. Matthias gave her an affectionate pat on the snout before retrieving the sword from her saddle.

As they made their way through the fortress, the halls of the Citadel buzzed with activity. Clerks hurried with stacks of parchment, and riders rushed about on various tasks, their expressions serious. It was as if war was imminent.

"What did we miss?" Evelyn asked.

"Your guess is as good as mine."

Matthias escorted Evelyn to the infirmary, then made his way to Curate Aric's office. Inside, Curate Aric stood at the head of a long table, its surface plastered with parchments and maps. His piercing eyes locked onto Matthias immediately, then flicked to the glowing sword in his hands.

"You've returned," Aric said. "Where's Evelyn?"

"She's in the infirmary. She'll be fine," he added as Aric's expression darkened. "She was injured but not by an enemy."

"I see. What's that?" he nodded toward the sword.

"If my information is correct, it's the only weapon that can stop the False King. We found it in the ruins of a place called Valen, but not without cost."

"Did you learn anything of Valerius's plans?"

"Yes. He's trying to craft a spell that will enslave dragons to do his bidding. He intends to invade Osnen and turn our dragons against us."

"How credible is this information?" Aric asked.

"The same person told me about this sword, and he was right. He was a servant who escaped Araphel."

Aric nodded. "I'll need to speak with Master Pevus about this. It doesn't bode well."

"If I may speak freely?"

"Of course."

"The time for defense has passed. We should strike at Midia with everything we have, take the fight to him and overwhelm his forces. If he manages to pull off that spell..." Matthias trailed off.

"I agree that we need to take action, but that's a decision for the council to make. I'll make your concerns known. Get some rest. You've earned it."

Matthias bowed his head and turned to leave.

"Leave the sword on the table," Aric said. "I want to make sure there's nothing about it that's going to work against us."

"As you command." Matthias set the sword on the table and left the room. He made his way to the infirmary to check on Evelyn, who was sitting up in bed as a healer tended to her leg. Her eyes met his, and she smiled.

"Hey," she said softly.

"Hey yourself," Matthias replied. "How are you feeling?"

"Better now that I'm not on my feet," Evelyn said with a wry smile. "Did you talk to Aric?"

"I did. He's going to share everything with the council. I was thinking of attending the meeting if you want to join me?"

Evelyn nodded.

"Good. I'll come get you before it starts. I'm going to try to sleep a little. You should do the same."

—

The council chamber was crowded with senior riders, Curates, and Master Pevus. It was warm and stuffy, and Matthias found the atmosphere suffocating. Evelyn sat at his side in a chair, her fatigue visible on her face. He was surprised she decided to attend the meeting.

Master Pevus surveyed the room with a sharp gaze. He was older, with gray hair and a beard to match. His years were etched into his face as deep lines, but his voice held the unyielding authority of a man who had carried Osnen through countless crises.

"We have heard Matthias's report," he began, his voice echoing off the chamber's walls. "Valerius, or the False King as he has come to be known, grows bolder. His dark magic threatens not only our people but the very balance of the world. If he succeeds in enslaving our dragons, Osnen will fall."

Murmurs broke out among the council members. Some argued in hushed tones, while others nodded grimly.

"Master," one of the Curates spoke up, his voice hesitant, "you speak of war, but the risks are great. To engage the enemy on his own soil could lead to great losses. Are we certain this is the best course of action?"

"That is a fair question, and one I have considered myself. Battling Midia's forces, whether here or there, will result in deaths that cannot be avoided. I believe launching an attack while Valerius is ill prepared will result in the least loss of life."

Another council member, a woman with streaks of gray in her auburn hair, leaned forward. "And what of our dragons? Will they be safe? If even one turns against us mid-battle, it could spell disaster."

"As far as we are aware, Valerius has not succeeded in taking control of a dragon," Master Pevus said. "The longer we wait heightens the chance that he'll succeed."

Curate Aric nodded, his expression grave. "You are right. Delay will cost us everything. The time has come to act. This council must decide: do we march into Midia and strike at the heart of this threat, or do we wait and risk annihilation?"

The chamber was silent for a long moment as the weight of the decision settled over everyone.

"I say we fight," Curate Anesko said.

Others nodded their agreement.

"We've been defending our borders for years, always reacting. It's time we take the fight to them," another Curate chimed in.

"All in favor?" Curate Aric asked.

Almost every hand rose.

"Then it is decided," Master Pevus declared. "The Dragon Guard will go to war. Every able-bodied rider must prepare. I will send word to the king."

11

THE CITADEL BUZZED WITH activity as the riders mobilized for the coming assault. The courtyard, which had been silent in the early dawn, now rang with the clang of hammers striking steel and the hurried shouts of soldiers preparing for battle. Rows of dragons lined the training grounds, their scales glinting in the rising sun as their riders fastened armor to their massive frames. The air was thick with the mingling scents of leather, oil, and dragon musk.

In less than two full days, every rider had been recalled from across Osnen. Matthias stood amidst the flurry of activity, his gaze fixed on Valkyra as she was being measured by a blacksmith.

I don't need this flimsy metal, Valkyra grumbled. *It weighs me down.*

It's for added protection, Matthias replied.

The dragon didn't complain further, but he could sense her displeasure through the bond as the smith and his assistants began fitting the armor on her.

With war looming, his thoughts turned to his wife and son. He wished he could see them before he left, but there wasn't time. They would be departing shortly, and Matthias knew he had to focus on the task at hand. He had a duty to protect his home and loved ones, even if it meant risking his life in battle.

He was pulled from his thoughts when Evelyn approached. "Have you eaten yet?" she asked.

Matthias shook his head. "I will. Later."

"You said that an hour ago." Evelyn's tone was light, but her eyes betrayed her concern.

"I've had a lot to do. I still have to check Valkyra's harness."

"Master Pevus is leading this endeavor, and he found time to eat." She nodded toward the main gates where he and the Curates were gathered.

He opened his mouth to argue but stopped when Valkyra's voice brushed against his mind. *She's right, you know. If you fall from exhaustion, you are no good to anyone.*

Matthias chuckled softly, shaking his head. "Even my dragon's against me now."

"Not against you," Evelyn said, her smile growing. "With you. Always."

The moment of levity was interrupted by Curate Aric's voice announcing they were departing soon.

"I wish I could go with you," Evelyn lamented. "I know I'm not a warrior, but my skills as a healer would be put to good use."

"You need to rest and let your leg heal. Besides, those who are injured will be returning here. You'll still be of help."

"Are you ready? For the battle, I mean."

"I don't think anyone can truly be ready for what's coming," Matthias admitted.

"You've proven yourself time and again. Trust in that. And trust in those who fight alongside you."

"I will. I'll see you when we return." Matthias made his way to Valkyra's side. The dragon stood tall, her blue scales gleaming like polished sapphires. He checked her saddle, which had been reinforced with additional straps to accommodate the armor.

Are you ready? Matthias ran a hand along Valkyra's snout.

I'm always ready.

Evelyn joined them and handed Matthias a wrapped package. "Here. Bread and dried meat. No excuses this time."

Matthias smirked but took the food. "Thanks."

As he ate a brief meal, the sounds of the Citadel's preparations filled the air. It was a symphony of war, and every note carried the weight of what lay ahead.

When the time came, Matthias climbed onto Valkyra's back, adjusting his position in the saddle. Valkyra spread her wings, the powerful muscles rippling beneath her scales, and with a mighty leap, she joined the other dragons taking to the sky. A chorus of roars erupted from the beasts, and Matthias felt a chill of excitement run through him. They soared beyond the Citadel, their formation heading north to Midia.

Matthias leaned forward on Valkyra's back, his gaze fixed on the horizon. The lead dragon, a massive green beast ridden by Master Pevus, directed the formation's movements. As the border came in sight, Matthias could see faint glimmers of light scattered across the mountainside— Midian outposts.

Those are new, he told Valkyra.

Curate Aric's voice echoed within his mind, amplified by the magical link shared by all dragon riders. *Do not engage unless ordered. Our goal is to cross unnoticed.*

The dragons shifted into a tighter formation, their powerful wings beating in unison as they passed the mountain. Matthias's pulse quickened as they slipped past the watchfires, their shadows fleeting and ghostlike. He clenched Valkyra's reins, every muscle in his body taut as he awaited the inevitable—an arrow, a battle cry, a horn blasting a warning.

But nothing happened.

As they crossed over a valley, the watchfires faded into the distance. The Dragon Guard had successfully crossed into Midian territory. The terrain below shifted from rugged peaks to rolling hills, and Matthias breathed easier.

That felt too easy.

Maybe they let us in, Valkyra replied.

Why would they do that?

They want us here.

Or they are afraid to stop us, Matthias said, though his tone carried little conviction.

As they pressed deeper into Midia, the hills gave way to desolate plains, the soil cracked and barren. Ahead, a black mountain rose from the earth like a shadow. Matthias knew Araphel was built upon the top of an extinct volcano, but seeing it in person sent a shiver down his spine. The dark fortress loomed ominously, its spires reaching for the sky like jagged claws. Around its base, a sprawling camp bustled with activity—Midian soldiers drilling in formation, tents pitched in neat rows, and siege weapons being readied.

Matthias's heart hammered in his chest as he took in the sheer scale of Valerius's forces. This was no mere outpost; it was a stronghold, a bastion of darkness that threatened to consume the land.

Prepare for battle, Curate Aric's voice echoed.

The dragons banked and began their descent just as a bell tower began clanging. The courtyard of the fortress erupted into chaos, and griffons took to the air.

They know we're here, Valkyra said.

Matthias unstrapped his crossbow from the saddle. There was no turning back now.

12

THE SKY BECAME A whirlwind of disorder. Dragons and griffons collided in brutal aerial combat, their roars and shrieks blending into a cacophony of sound. The clash was fierce. Fire spewed from open jaws, painting the sky in a kaleidoscope of destruction.

Hold on! Valkyra shouted as she dove toward an oncoming griffon rider. She unleashed a torrent of flames, and the griffon shrieked in pain, its rider flailing before tumbling from the saddle.

Matthias raised his crossbow and fired, the bolt piercing another rider in the shoulder. His griffon faltered, veering away from the fight. Valkyra darted through the fray, dodging strikes and returning them with precision. The battle blurred into a series of moments—fire and steel, cries of triumph and pain.

Below in the courtyard, a robed figure raised a staff, releasing a pulse of dark magic that surged outward. The effect was immediate and devastating. Some of the dragons hesitated, their movements erratic. Others turned on their riders, their eyes glowing with an unnatural green light.

Matthias's heart sank as he watched one of his comrades struggle against their own dragon, the beast snapping and snarling as if possessed. Dread coiled around him as he considered how to fend off Valkyra.

Is the spell affecting you?

No, Valkyra replied. *Others are not so fortunate.*

Even from a distance, Matthias could feel the oppressive weight of the magic, a malevolent force that seemed to drain the very air of life.

We have to stop him! Matthias yelled.

I agree, but that's easier said than done.

The figure in the courtyard continued his spell, the dark magic spreading like a plague.

We need to confront him directly.

Breaking through the enemy lines is no small feat, Valkyra argued.

We will fight our way to him.

Valkyra rumbled, her concerns flowing through the bond. *You'll need the sword. Who has it?*

Before Matthias could reply, he watched in horror as a group of griffons attacked Curate Aric, overwhelming his dragon.

He does, Matthias said.

Valkyra's powerful wings beat against the air as she cut through the chaos of battle toward the endangered Curate. The wind whipped past them as they closed in on the griffons, who were focused solely on their target. With a mighty roar, Valkyra breathed a stream of scorching flames at the lead griffon, causing it to veer off course with a piercing screech. Matthias seized the opportunity and leaned forward, firing his crossbow. The bolt found its mark and punched a hole through a second griffon's wing.

Aric's dragon fought valiantly, deflecting strikes and unleashing bursts of flame, but the griffons were relentless, their talons slashing and beaks snapping. Valkyra angled sharply, snatching a griffon up in one claw while she whipped her tail into another.

"The sword!" Matthias shouted at Curate Aric. "Where's the sword?"

Aric pulled the blade from the saddle and attempted to hurl it, but his dragon jerked away from a strike and the sword went flying askew, twirling downward end over end. Valkyra dove after the weapon.

Below, the robed figure with the staff retreated inside the castle. The ground quaked, and shadows writhed like living things. The roar of battle faltered as confusion spread through the Osnen ranks. Some dragons froze mid-flight, their wings folding awkwardly as they spiraled toward the ground. Others turned on their riders, their eyes blazing with a sickly green glow.

A squadron of dragons began tearing into one another, their massive bodies thrashing as their riders screamed in vain, struggling to regain control.

It's spreading, Matthias said, his voice tight with dread. His focus turned to Valkyra. *Are you still with me?*

For now... the pressure is growing.

Matthias could hear the strain in her voice. Their bond was growing thin, disintegrating under the magic. The wind roared as Valkyra tucked her wings close to her body, cutting through the air at impossible speed to reach the sword.

The weapon struck the ground point first, embedding itself in the earth. Valkyra didn't let up, and Matthias realized her body had gone limp.

Valkyra! he screamed. *Valkyra!*

She struck the ground hard, sending up a spray of earth and debris. Matthias was flung from the saddle, rolling across the unforgiving terrain until he came to a stop. Pain exploded through him, every nerve and muscle screaming in protest. He lay there in shock, staring up at the chaos unfolding in the sky.

The battle had devolved into madness. The magic continued to spread, infecting everything it touched. Matthias's heart seized with fear for Valkyra. He staggered to his feet, ignoring the pain that flared in his limbs. His vision blurred as he staggered toward his dragon.

She lay motionless on the ground, her powerful wings splayed out at odd angles. Desperation clawed at his chest as he rushed to her side and dropped to his knees beside her. His hands shook as he reached out to touch her side. No warmth greeted him, no reassuring hum of life beneath his fingers.

"Valkyra," he whispered aloud, his eyes full of tears. "Please, don't leave me."

He choked with grief. The battle continued to rage around him, but Matthias felt as if the world had shrunk to encompass only him and his fallen companion. Tears streamed down his cheeks as he cradled Valkyra's massive head in his lap, her eyes fixed and unseeing.

"I failed you."

Matthias bowed his head and wept, the weight of defeat pressing down on him with unbearable force. He had lost not only a companion but a friend. Their bond had transcended mere words, and the enormity of Valkyra's death settled over him like a heavy shroud.

The echo of Aric's voice cut through his despair.

Riders, to me!

Matthias looked up and saw Curate Aric rallying those whose dragons had not succumbed to the dark magic. He stood as a beacon of hope against the darkness. Matthias's grief burned away as rage took its place.

He staggered to his feet, the pain in his body forgotten. Without Valkyra by his side, he would have to find another way to confront the enemy. He looked around for the sword of Valen, his eyes landing on the blade buried in the earth not far from where Valkyra lay.

Matthias strode to it and wrenched it from the ground. Each step was a battle against the grief threatening to consume him, but he pushed it down, burying it as deep as he could. He turned his gaze to the fortress of Araphel and clenched his jaw.

He was going to kill the False King.

13

THE FORTRESS LOOMED LIKE a monstrous beast against the darkening sky. From this distance, the cries of battle and the clash of steel faded into a dull roar, leaving Matthias in a bubble of silence broken only by the wind.

The gates had been shattered in the earlier assault, twisted and hanging from their hinges like the ribs of some long-dead beast. He stepped cautiously inside, his boots crunching against the debris littering the entryway. The stench of sulfur and decay greeted him, a reminder of the foul magic that ravaged the sky.

The courtyard was eerily quiet, the only sound the faint crackle of distant flames and the occasional rumble as the ground trembled, the result of a dragon falling from the sky. Shadows seemed to writhe along the walls, unnatural in their movements.

The shadows thickened as he entered the fortress, and a chill ran down his spine.

Whispered voices began to fill the air, faint at first but growing louder with each step.

"Matthias..."

He froze. The voice was unmistakable—his wife's.

"How could you abandon us?"

His throat tightened, but he forced himself to move forward. The whispers twisted, becoming his son's voice, then Valkyra's, all accusing him of failure.

"You'll fail them, just as you failed us," the voices hissed.

"Enough!" Matthias shouted, the sword flaring with light.

The shadows recoiled, retreating to the edges of the hall. The whispers faded, replaced by an oppressive silence. Matthias pressed on, his heart pounding in his chest. He could feel the fortress itself resisting his presence, as if the False King's magic had made the very stones hostile to intruders.

At last, he reached a massive set of double doors, their surfaces engraved with runes that pulsed faintly with malevolent energy. Matthias took a deep breath and placed a hand on the doors. With a powerful push, they swung open, revealing the shadowed throne room beyond.

It was a cavernous expanse, its walls draped in shadows cast by the flickering light of braziers. The air was humid and thick with the acrid tang of something he couldn't quite place, making each breath a struggle. At the far end of the room, the False King sat upon a throne of black stone, its jagged edges seemingly carved from the bones of some creature.

He rose as Matthias entered, his long cloak trailing behind him like a shadow come to life. Valerius Draven was tall and hearty, his body covered in dark armor etched with runes that glowed with a red tinge. His eyes burned with malevolence, twin orbs of cold fire that pierced the dimness of the room.

"What do we have here?" Valerius said, his voice booming. "Someone with a death wish?"

Matthias stepped forward, the sword of Valen pulsing with a light that seemed to push back against the oppressive darkness. "I've come to end your reign of terror. Free the dragons from your vile magic."

Valerius laughed, a hollow sound that chilled Matthias to the core. "Free them? They are mine, bound by powers far greater than your pitiful blade. Do you think a relic of a forgotten age will save you?"

"You *will* release them," Matthias replied, his voice firm despite the fear coiling in his chest.

"Let us see if you are worthy of the blade you wield."

Valerius raised his hand, and tendrils of shadow snaked across the floor toward Matthias, whipping toward him with the speed of striking vipers. He sidestepped the first and brought the sword down on the second, its light severing the shadowy appendage with a hiss.

Matthias charged, his blade aimed at the Valeriu's heart, but the man unsheathed his own sword and unleashed a torrent of green fire from the tip of the blade. Matthias raised weapon just in time, its light creating a shimmering shield that absorbed the flames.

"Impressive," Valerius sneered. "But I cannot be bested by brute force."

He stabbed his sword into the ground, and the throne room shifted. The floor cracked and splintered, sending jagged pillars of stone shooting up around Matthias, cutting off his path. The shadows moved again, forming spectral figures that lunged at him with ethereal weapons.

Matthias spun, cutting through the phantoms as they charged. Each swing of the blade sent arcs of light through the room, momentarily dispelling the darkness. But for every phantom he struck down, another took its place.

Valerius advanced slowly, his sword radiating energy. "Do you see now? You cannot win. My power is endless, my will unbreakable."

Matthias's breath came in ragged gasps as he fought, his arms burning with exertion. The room seemed to close in around him, the oppressive weight threatening to crush his resolve.

"Do you feel it yet?" Valerius taunted, his voice echoing from every corner of the room. "The weight of despair? The futility of your struggle?"

The sword flared, and he suddenly remembered the trials of Valen—the fear he had faced, the lessons he had learned. He was not the man who had entered those ruins, uncertain and afraid. He was stronger now.

Matthias steadied his stance and surged forward, weaving through the onslaught of shadowy tendrils and lunging at Valerius. The usurper deflected the attack with his sword, the clash of light and dark sending shockwaves through the chamber.

"You may be powerful," Matthias said, his voice rising above the din, "but you are not invincible."

Valerius snarled, stabbing his sword into the ground again, sending out a wave of sickly green energy that struck Matthias square in the chest. He was hurled backward, landing hard on the cold, cracked floor. The sword of Valen skittered out of his grip, its glow dimming as it spun away.

"You cannot win," the False King hissed, his voice layered with an unnatural echo. "You believe you can because that is the delusion of hope. I will crush it from you, and from anyone else who stands in my way."

The room darkened further until Matthias couldn't see the walls or ceiling, only an endless void. Shadows coiled and shifted, forming into vague shapes that gradually became clearer. Matthias froze as he recognized the figures before him. His loved ones—his wife, son, and

Valkyra—stood in a circle of pale light. Their faces were drawn with fear, their bodies frail and trembling. Behind them loomed monstrous shapes, their shadows reaching out to engulf them.

"Matthias," his wife called out, her voice small and trembling. "Help us!"

Matthias tried to rise, but his legs felt as though they were weighed down by iron chains. The shadows moved closer to his family, their twisted forms laughing with cruel, echoing voices.

"You couldn't save your dragon," Valerius's voice sneered, reverberating through the void. "You'll fail your family, too. No matter how strong you think you are, you can't protect anyone. Like everyone else, you will run from my flames."

Matthias clenched his fists. The image of Valkyra's lifeless body lying on the ground overwhelmed him with a sense of helplessness. The shadows swirled faster, their claws inches from his son's shoulder. Matthias's heart thundered in his chest as doubt clawed at him. But then, through the cacophony of voices, another memory surfaced: Evelyn's voice as she spoke to him before he left the Citadel.

"You are more than your fears, Matthias. You've faced them before, and you've risen stronger every time."

The words lit a spark in his mind, and he remembered every challenge he'd overcome, every trial that had brought him to this moment. He had survived. He had endured. And now, he had the power to make a difference.

The chains holding him down shattered as Matthias forced himself to his feet. The sword of Valen, lying a few feet away, began to glow stronger as if responding to his determination.

"You're wrong," Matthias said. "I'm not a man who runs from the flames. I'm the man who stands against them."

The shadows hesitated, their laughter faltering.

Matthias strode toward the sword, each step dispelling the darkness around him. He grabbed it off the ground, its light flaring to life and banishing the remaining shadows. The figures of his family dissolved into wisps of light, their faces calm and unburdened. The void receded, replaced by the cracked stone floor of the throne room.

Valerius stood at the far end of the room, his eyes narrowing in fury. "You think a spark of courage will save you?" he spat.

Matthias raised the sword of Valen, its glow unwavering. "It already has."

Valerius raised his sword, the dark energy gathering once more. But this time, Matthias stood tall, the light of his own blade casting away the shadows with every step forward. He was no longer weighed down by fear. He was ready to face the darkness head-on, no matter the cost.

Matthias charged, and the two met in the center of the room, steel and magic colliding. Matthias ducked under a sweep of Valerius's sword and swung his blade upward, forcing him to stumble back.

Valerius lashed out with a bolt of raw magic, striking Matthias's shoulder. Searing agony shot through his body. He staggered back, clenching his jaw against the pain. His grip on the sword tightened, and he pushed forward, each step fueled by the thought of those he sought to protect.

With the last of his strength, Matthias lunged. Valerius raised his blade to block the strike, but Matthias's sword shattered it in two.

The False King screamed, the sound inhuman and filled with rage. His dark magic lashed out uncontrollably, tearing apart the room around them.

Matthias took advantage of the moment, driving his blade straight into Valerius's stomach. The blade sank deep, its light exploding outward. The False King's scream turned to a gurgle as the dark magic surrounding him began to dissolve.

"You... cannot... stop me..." Valerius rasped, his eyes wide with fury and disbelief. "Even in death, the darkness will rise again..."

Matthias twisted the blade, silencing him.

Valerius's body sank to the floor. Matthias stood over him, chest heaving. The sword still glowed faintly in his grip, but its light dimmed with the threat gone. Around him, the fortress began to tremble violently. The walls cracked, and pieces of the ceiling began to rain down. Dust billowed into the air, thickening until it stung his eyes and clawed at his throat.

He turned toward the exit but froze when he saw the destruction unfolding. An enormous slab of stone broke free, slamming into the floor and cutting off his path. Without warning, the floor gave way, crumbling like dry bread underfoot. Matthias threw himself forward, rolling as the ground splintered and swallowed itself behind him.

He rose to his knees and looked for another way out, but it was too late. The entire room was collapsing in on itself. Crawling to where the exit was, his hands scrambled against the cold stones, pushing, pulling, searching for a weakness, but the rocks did not yield, and the fortress continued its relentless descent into ruin.

His gaze swept the ruins, and there, he glimpsed a faint glimmer of hope—a narrow crevice, barely wide enough to squeeze through. He scrambled into the gap, contorting his body to fit inside the slender opening. The stones pressed close, threatening to crush him with their weight.

Matthias grunted, muscles straining against the unyielding stone. Darkness clawed at his vision, but Matthias pushed onward, driven by the thought of open skies and the chance to breathe.

Yet, as he wriggled desperately, the rocks above shifted, sealing shut the sliver of escape. Matthias froze. He was trapped—truly trapped. The tremors ceased, leaving behind a dreadful stillness. As the last of the sound faded, so too did the strength from his limbs.

The fortress, with its dying breath, had claimed him as its own.

14

THE FIRST OF THE surviving riders arrived at the Citadel, their heads low and their dragons weak with exhaustion. The setting sun cast a golden glow over the courtyard, a sharp contrast to the soot-stained armor and battle-worn expressions of those returning.

Evelyn pushed through the crowd, desperate for a glimpse of Matthias's tall frame or the gleam of Valkyra's blue scales. When the final dragon landed, she realized Matthias was not among them.

The crowd that was gathered in the square erupted into cheers. The noise grated against Evelyn's ears, a cruel mockery of the loss that hung like a shroud over the survivors. There were many missing dragons, and many more saddles empty of familiar faces.

Master Pevus strode to the front of the crowd with deliberate slowness, his presence commanding instant attention. He raised his hands, calling for silence. The cheering ceased, replaced by a tense hush. All eyes turned to him.

"This day," Pevus began, his tone heavy with sorrow, "is one of both triumph and tragedy. We have won the battle. Valerius Draven, the False King, has fallen, and his dark reign has ended. For that, we must give thanks to the bravery of the Dragon Guard, the valor of our dragons, and the sacrifices of those who fought by our side."

His words hung in the air.

"But this triumph did not come without a price," he continued, his voice breaking slightly. "We have lost many of our own—friends, comrades, family. And among those fallen is Matthias Baines, the one who struck the final blow against the False King."

A ripple of shock spread through the crowd. Gasps and murmurs echoed off the stone walls, and Evelyn felt the air leave her lungs.

"Matthias," Pevus said, his voice steady once more, "gave his life to free our dragons and end the False King's dark magic. He stood alone in the heart of the enemy's fortress, knowing full well the cost of his actions. He died so that we might live, and so that our kingdom would remain free."

Tears blurred Evelyn's vision as she turned away, unable to bear the words any longer.

"Let his name be remembered," Pevus declared, his voice rising with conviction. "Let it be sung in every hall, in every home. Let our children and their children know the courage of Matthias. He died a hero, and his sacrifice will live on in the hearts of all who fight for freedom. As we celebrate this victory, let us also mourn those we have lost. Let us carry their memory with us, not as a burden but as a guiding light. Their sacrifice was not in vain. We live because of them. Osnen stands because of them."

A solemn silence settled over the courtyard. No cheers followed this speech, only the sound of the wind whispering through the battlements. Evelyn turned and pushed her way through the crowd, her chest tightening with each step.

When she finally broke free of the throng, she stumbled into the shadows of the lower courtyard, her legs trembling. The weight of grief pressed down on her, threatening to crush her entirely. She bit her lip until it bled, trying to stifle the sobs that clawed their way up her throat, but it was no use. Matthias was gone.

And the world, despite their victory, felt unbearably empty without him.

—

The late afternoon sun bathed the Citadel as Curate Aric prepared for his journey. He stood in the armory, his hands methodically checking his travel gear. His dark blue robes, embroidered with silver threads that marked his station, had been freshly cleaned, though a faint crease in the fabric hinted at the tension he carried.

On the table before him lay a scroll, sealed with the royal crest of Osnen. The words within carried the weight of a kingdom's gratitude: a declaration granting Matthias and his family the title of Noble by Deed, elevating his name to one that would be remembered for generations to come.

Aric's fingers hovered over the scroll, his chest tight. He had delivered grim news many times in his role, but this task felt heavier than any before. He would not only be informing a widow of her husband's heroic death but also placing the burden of his legacy upon her and their child.

A knock at the door drew his attention. Master Pevus entered, his expression solemn. "Do you want me to come with you?"

Aric shook his head. "This is something I must do alone."

Master Pevus nodded, though his eyes betrayed his concern. "The roads are quiet for now, but take care. Valerius may be dead, but his followers won't vanish overnight."

"I'll be careful," Aric assured him. He secured the scroll in a leather case and slung it over his shoulder. After exchanging a brief clasp of hands with Master Pevus, he left the armory and made his way to the stables.

His horse, a sturdy bay mare named Lyria, was already saddled and waiting. The stablemaster handed him the reins with a quiet word of encouragement, and Aric mounted smoothly. He glanced back at the Citadel, its spires glinting in the sunlight, before urging Lyria into a steady trot.

The journey to Matthias's home was long, the path winding through rolling hills and dense forests. Aric's mind wandered as he rode, the rhythmic clip of hooves on the dirt road offering a strange solace. He thought of

Matthias—the man who had stood tall against impossible odds.

By the time Aric reached the outskirts of Matthias's village, the sun was dipping below the horizon, painting the sky in hues of orange and crimson. Smoke rose lazily from chimneys, and the faint sound of children's laughter carried on the breeze.

The Baines' house was modest but well-kept, nestled at the edge of the village with a small garden out front. Aric dismounted and tied Lyria to a post, taking a moment to steady himself before approaching the door. He adjusted the leather strap of his satchel, which contained Matthias's personal effects to be returned.

Inhaling a deep breath, he knocked gently, the sound echoing in the quiet evening. Moments later, the door opened, and Matthias's wife, Lena, appeared. Her dark hair was tied back, and her face, though marked by lines of hard work, carried a quiet strength.

"Curate Aric," she greeted, her tone polite but curious. "What brings you here?"

"May I come in?" Aric asked softly.

Lena stepped aside, ushering him in. A small table sat in the center of the room, and the scent of stew lingered in the air. A boy of no more than eight years old—Eldwin, Matthias's son—peered at Aric from behind a chair, his wide eyes filled with curiosity.

Aric removed the scroll case from his shoulder, cradling it in his hands as he turned to Lena. "I bring news," he began, his voice steady despite the ache in his chest. "Matthias... he fought bravely. He gave his life to save us all and to ensure the False King's reign would end."

Lena's breath caught, her hand flying to her mouth. Her knees buckled, and she collapsed into a nearby chair. Aric knelt before her, setting the case on the table and placing a reassuring hand on hers.

"I am so sorry for your loss," he said. "But know this—Matthias died a hero. He gave his life to protect Osnen, to protect you and your son."

Tears streamed down Lena's face, but she managed a trembling nod. Eldwin stepped forward, his small hands clutching the back of the chair for support. His expression was a mix of confusion and dawning realization.

Aric opened the case and withdrew the scroll, handing it to Lena. "This is a declaration from the king," he explained. "In recognition of Matthias's bravery and sacrifice, your family has been granted the title of Noble by Deed. You and Eldwin are now part of Osnen's nobility."

Lena accepted the scroll with trembling hands, her eyes scanning the elegant script. "He... he always wanted to do something meaningful," she whispered. "And he did."

Aric rose to his feet, his gaze shifting to Eldwin. "Your father was a great man," he said. "You should be proud of him."

Eldwin met Aric's eyes, his small fists clenched at his sides. "I am," he replied, his voice quiet. "And one day, I'll be a dragon rider like him. I'll... I'll be brave like him."

A lump formed in Aric's throat, but he managed a nod. "I believe you will, Eldwin."

He turned back to Lena, inclining his head respectfully. "If you ever need anything, the Citadel will always be here for you."

Lena managed a weak smile through her tears. "Thank you, Curate."

Aric stepped outside, the cool evening air filling his lungs. He mounted Lyria and took one last look at the house before urging her into a trot. As he rode away, he couldn't shake the image of Eldwin's determined face.

"Matthias," he murmured under his breath, "your legacy will live on—in more ways than one."

15

THE SUN DIPPED BELOW the horizon, leaving the small house in shadows. Inside, the room was silent except for the soft crackling of the fire in the hearth. Lena sat at the table, the royal scroll clutched in her trembling hands. Her tears had dried, leaving faint streaks on her cheeks, but her eyes remained fixed on the words that declared her husband a hero of Osnen.

Eldwin stood near the door, staring out at the fading light of the evening. His young face, usually bright with curiosity, was now etched with a maturity far beyond his years. His small hands were clenched into fists at his sides, his knuckles white.

He could still hear Curate Aric's words echoing in his mind: *"Your father was a great man."*

His father. Gone.

Eldwin closed his eyes, a lump rising in his throat. He had always thought of his father as invincible—a man who could do anything, who could protect them from any danger. Now, the realization of his father's sacrifice weighed heavily on him, filling his chest with a mixture of pride and unbearable grief.

He turned back to his mother, who sat silently, lost in her thoughts. The scroll lay open on the table, the flickering firelight dancing across the royal crest at the top. Eldwin stepped closer, his gaze fixed on the parchment.

"Mother," he said, his voice soft but steady.

Lena looked up, startled out of her reverie. Her red-rimmed eyes met her son's, and she managed a weak smile. "Yes, my love?"

Eldwin hesitated for a moment, his small frame trembling. But then he straightened his back, his youthful determination shining through.

"I'm going to be a dragon rider," he declared, his voice firm.

For a moment, she didn't respond. She opened her mouth to speak, to tell him that he was too young, that it was too dangerous, but the look in his eyes stopped her. He wasn't a child making an impulsive decision. He was her son, Matthias's son, and the conviction in his gaze reminded her so much of her husband that it took her breath away.

"You are?" she asked softly, her voice breaking.

Eldwin nodded, stepping closer to the table. He reached out and placed his hand on the scroll, his small fingers brushing against the words that honored his father's sacrifice.

"I'll train. I'll do whatever it takes," he continued, his voice growing stronger with each word. "I'll make him proud. I'll make both of you proud."

Lena's heart ached as she watched him, torn between wanting to protect him and knowing that she couldn't hold him back. She reached out and pulled him into her arms, holding him tightly.

"You already make me proud, my sweet boy," she whispered into his hair.

Eldwin hugged her back, his resolve hardening. When she finally released him, he stepped back, his eyes shining with unshed tears.

"I'll be the best dragon rider Osnen has ever seen," he vowed. "And I'll make sure everyone remembers what father did—for all of us."

Lena nodded, her throat too tight to speak. She watched as her son turned and walked to the door, standing in its frame as he gazed out at the evening sky.

Above, the first stars began to appear, twinkling faintly against the deep indigo. Eldwin tilted his head back, his eyes searching the heavens as though seeking his father's spirit among the constellations.

"I promise, father," he whispered, his words carried away by the evening breeze. "I'll honor your name. I'll make you proud."

And with that, the boy who had lost his father began to forge a path that would ensure Matthias's legacy lived on, not just in the songs of the people but also in his heart.

THE END

ABOUT THE AUTHOR

Richard Fierce is an award-winning author of over 40 books. You can find more information about him, his books, and his appearances at his website: www.richardfierce.com

www.ingramcontent.com/pod-product-compliance
Lightning Source LLC
Chambersburg PA
CBHW020046310726
48970CB00007B/2437